Who's in charge of Lincoln?

Who *was* in charge of Lincoln? Everything was arranged in case Lincoln's mother had to go to the hospital early. But when she did, the plans got confused and Lincoln was left in their New York apartment with no one to look after him.

What took place during the next two days surpassed anything Lincoln could imagine on his own — and he was good at that. But even Lincoln could never have guessed what would happen and where he would go when a bag of suspicious money fell into his hands.

Dale Fife's marvelous sense of humor has created a wonderful character in Lincoln Farnum, age eight.

Who's in charge

Illustrated by Paul Galdone

COWARD-McCANN, INC.   New York

of Lincoln?

y DALE FIFE

To CAMILLE with love

Who's in charge of Lincoln?

1

No ONE BELIEVED the things that happened to Lincoln.

Not his big sister Sara.

Not his middle-sized sisters, Sassy and Sissy.

Even Pop sometimes raised an eyebrow at Lincoln's stories.

Mom always listened with a serious face to whatever Lincoln had to tell.

But Mom had to leave suddenly for the hospital early this morning to bring home the new baby who it seemed was joining the Farnums two days early.

This put the family smack in the middle of the emergency Pop had worried about, and now no one believed Lincoln when he announced that a horse had fallen on Mrs. Readywell.

Pop had the family organized and running as smoothly as his railroad. "Always start with a clear track, and an eagle-eyed engineer who knows how to get where he's going," was his favorite advice. Before Pop left last night on his New York-to-Chicago run, he wrote out Emergency Orders.

So here they were, the four Farnums, lined up in the kitchen like a string of boxcars, with Sara the acting "Eagle Eyes." Her voice, as she read Pop's instructions, was real bossy:

> "In case your mother should go to the hospital while I'm away, Sassy and Sissy are to go straight to Aunt Charlotte's from school, with NO BRANCHING OFF the main line. They are to stay until I get home so Sara will be free to go with her class to Washington."

Sassy and Sissy jumped up and down, excited about staying overnight at Aunt Charlotte's.

Lincoln thought about Sara going to Washington, Mr. Lincoln's city. Pop and Mom had gone a year ago. So had Uncle Jay. They still talked about it. What stories they told. Lincoln liked to listen to them.

And Sara was going there this very day. She was in charge of the family this morning and acting as important as a switch engine in a roundhouse, but just the same her eyes danced and she looked pretty in her best dress.

"May I go with you, Sara?" Lincoln asked, knowing the answer full well.

"Of course not," the know-it-all twin, Sassy, flared. "It's mostly high school students who get to go in a group. You're just a little third-grader. Much too young."

"I'm not," Lincoln protested.

"Who's in charge of Lincoln?" Sissy, the curious twin, asked.

"If you'll all hush," Sara said, "I'll read the rest of the instructions:

"Lincoln is to come home from school as usual. Mrs. Readywell will be here."

"Why doesn't Lincoln go with us?" Sissy asked.

"Because he's a boy and Aunt Charlotte has only girls

11

and boys make her nervous," Sara said. "Especially boys who get lost for hours on end."

"I wasn't lost that time at Aunt Charlotte's," Lincoln said. "I was up on the apartment roof looking through my telescope, watching the people on Mars."

Sara sighed and went on talking. "Mrs. Readywell was coming anyway to stay while Mom was in the hospital. Pop asked her to come earlier, just in case. Won't she be surprised when she gets here today and finds Mom's already left?"

Lincoln raised his voice once more. "A horse fell on Mrs. Readywell."

Sissy giggled. "Lincoln's dreaming again."

"It's his imagination blasting off," Sassy said. "Ten . . . nine . . . eight . . ."

"Quiet, everyone," Sara ordered. "It's time to get yourselves ready for school."

Girls! Lincoln thought. You just couldn't tell them anything. They knew it all. Well, there was one thing they didn't know. A horse *did* fall on Mrs. Readywell.

2

IN HIS ROOM, which was at the front of the apartment, Lincoln stuffed his books into his book bag. He made his bed, pounding the lumps flat with his fists, and he straightened the statue of Mr. Lincoln which stood on his bookshelf.

Mr. Lincoln was his special friend. It was true that Lincoln sometimes mixed the real with the dreams. Living in a house noisy with girl talk, he had to. Now Mr. Lincoln was real, but not real-real like this red brick apartment. It wasn't a big apartment house, just three floors with two families on each floor. Some of the older people called it a flat, and it stood in a long row of buildings all just like it. The rooms marched in a straight line like a string of cars on Pop's railroad, and so Lincoln sometimes pretended he was on a train.

Lincoln knew about trains because Pop talked to him about his work. Just last month Pop took him on the subway to the railroad station and showed him all around the yards, and let him climb aboard and walk through a mainline passenger train, from one end to the other.

Lincoln looked out the window onto the street and saw that the fat girl with the long braids was twisting again. Now, *she* was real. She was the very last of the hoopers on the block. Whenever Lincoln looked out the window she was there twisting in her red hoop.

The girls having a quick game of hopscotch before school in the spring sunshine, they were real, and the boys bouncing a ball off the sooty flat across the street. And Officer Roberts, talking with the ladies on the stoop across the street, he was real.

The telephone call from Mrs. Readywell this morning was real too. Mom had come out into the kitchen with her coat and hat on, and carrying a little suitcase. Sara had

15

rushed out to hail a cab. Everyone had been excited and gone with Mom out to the street and helped her into the cab. She was giving all kinds of last-minute instructions: "Lincoln, you be polite to Mrs. Readywell; Sara, you call Aunt Charlotte, and be careful in Washington; Sissy and Sassy, you mind Aunt Charlotte . . ."

In all the confusion, with the cab pulling away from the curb and everyone shouting good-bye, Lincoln was the only one who heard the telephone ring. As soon as he answered, Mrs. Readywell began talking as if he were Mom: "A saw-horse fell on me while I was painting the bathroom just now. It was standing on end in the corner and it toppled over and broke my glasses. It's not enough that I have a tin ear; now I can't see either. So I won't be able to come today because I have to get new glasses. I'll be there to-morrow afternoon, and don't you get any ideas about going to the hospital early."

Mrs. Readywell had hung up before Lincoln could tell her that Mom was already on the way to the hospital. It wouldn't have done any good anyway. Mrs. Readywell

couldn't hear well and a conversation with her was just one-way.

Across the street now Officer Roberts smiled good-bye to the ladies on the stoop and headed for the subway corner. Lincoln slung his book bag over his shoulder and ran the length of the apartment from the engine to the caboose.

From the rear window nothing was real. The scraggly tree growing out of the little concrete square next to the basement was a palm in a steaming jungle, and the two tomcats, who ruled from clothesline and fence, were ferocious tigers. The basketball standard which Pop and Uncle Jay had put up for Lincoln stood tall as a giraffe.

Lincoln pushed back his pith helmet and began cranking his movie camera.

"Lincoln!" It was Sara. "Bring the peanut butter please."

Reluctantly, Lincoln left the safari and brought Sara the peanut butter. He watched her make sandwiches. "Tell me about Washington again," he said.

"Well, our class has been saving money for three years to go. You remember, we had that rummage sale, and the boys washed cars in the summer, and shoveled snow in the winter, and the girls made candy to sell. Well, now our bank account is fat and it's almost the end of the school year

18

and we're going on a special excursion train this afternoon after school. We'll be away the whole weekend."

When Sara talked to Lincoln like this, he didn't mind that she was a girl and often bossy. Of course, he'd much rather have a brother because a boy could talk to a brother all the time, not just once in a while. Girls usually wanted to talk about silly things like clothes and hair. But this morning Sara was all right.

"Will you see Mr. Lincoln?" he asked.

"We'll visit the Lincoln Memorial of course, and places like Ford's Theatre, and the Smithsonian Institution, and we'll see Mount Vernon."

"I'd want to see Mr. Lincoln first of all," Lincoln said. "Where you going first?"

"The White House probably because it's open to tourists only until noon."

"You going right in?"

"Of course. Anyone can. All you need to do is get into line. The White House belongs to us."

"To me?"

"Yes. Washington belongs to the people."

"Then why do you have to have money?"

"Expenses."

Lincoln thought about this while he scooped up a spoonful of peanut butter and let the nutty taste melt in his mouth. "Tell me about my bedroom."

Sara smiled a him. "Abraham Lincoln's bedroom."

"When will I see it?"

"Oh, in about eight years."

Eight years! How could he wait that long? If he were named Ed or Bill or Winston it wouldn't be so important to him to go. But he was Lincoln. Whenever he told his name, someone was sure to say: "That's a fine name. The greatest." It wasn't half as important for a girl with the name of Sara to go to Washington as it was for a boy by the name of Lincoln.

When Pop and Mom and Uncle Jay went to Washington, they brought Sissy and Sassy and Sara bright scarves and new pocketbooks. But they brought Lincoln his statue of the President and a book about him. Why, Lincoln was even planning to be a lawyer like the President. Maybe he'd start out the same way in a long cabin . . .

"Okay everyone," Sara cried, jerking Lincoln right out of the log cabin and back into the kitchen where she was bagging the sandwiches. "Pick up your lunches. Time for school."

Lincoln thought she sounded just like a railroad conductor calling: "All Aboard."

She gave him one of her bossiest looks. "Remember to come straight home. Mrs. Readywell will be waiting."

"No she won't. A horse fell on her."

Sara sighed. "Just you come straight home, as usual."

"Yes, ma'am!"

3

LINCOLN SCOOTED OUT of the apartment ahead of Sissy and Sassy. It wasn't any fun walking to school with them. They talked and talked and never saw a thing.

Looking down the street, the apartments seemed all alike, but when you took time to notice, each one had a different face.

The one next door was empty. The green shades were pulled way down and old newspapers littered the stoop. Lincoln thought maybe it was haunted and he hurried along to the next one.

Mrs. Krutznitt's apartment had a happy face. The shades were pulled right to the top of the windows to let in the sun. Mrs. Krutznitt was very old and she was sitting in the window, her head nodding. With each nod her glasses slipped a little farther down her nose. Lincoln watched to see if this time they would fall clear off. But Mrs. Krutznitt jerked awake just in time to catch them. Lincoln grinned. Mrs. Krutznitt smiled and waved.

Next door, a pink rose bloomed on Mrs. Ortega's windowsill. Lincoln knew it was plastic and had come with a bag of potato chips, but it looked so real he could smell it.

Down the street a new sound came from Mrs. Jones' stoop. Mrs. Jones stood in her doorway smiling and pointing to the tinkling music. "Temple bells. I bought them in Woolworth's," she said. Lincoln stood still, listening to the mysterious glass-on-glass sound. Suddenly he was in the temple of a faraway land. He heard the cymbals, smelled the incense and saw the golden dragons. Until a boy bumped into him, which put Lincoln right back on his street.

At the corner Lincoln turned around to see if Sissy and Sassy were following him. They weren't in sight yet so he made a quick right turn. He thought he'd like to have a look at the new apartment going up around the block. He had to be sure the girls didn't see him or they'd start yelling: "You'll be late for school. We'll tell Pop."

That's the way girls were and a boy couldn't do a thing about it. Now Herman would be different. From the very first, when Lincoln learned the new baby was coming, he had named it Herman. He thought Herman had just the right sound for a boy who would be strong and fearless and not cute-cute. You could play all kinds of games with a Herman: Herman, the Gladiator; Herman, the Knight of the Round Table; Herman, the Astronaut.

Mom kept saying: "Maybe we'll call the baby Hermione."

But Lincoln didn't believe the family could be that unlucky. They already had three girls and there wasn't room for any more dresses in the closets. Besides, he had already divided his toys, half for Herman and half for himself. What would a girl do with six marbles, a dump truck, and a catcher's mitt?

As soon as Lincoln turned the next corner he saw that the tall apartment was almost finished. It was shining white, and it had a glass door and a brass doorknob. Standing in between two old brick buildings it looked so pretty and newborn. Kind of like Herman.

The sidewalk in front of the apartment was newly made.

A rope barrier kept people from stepping on it, so Lincoln walked in the street to reach the other side. The roped-off square reminded Lincoln of pictures he had seen of that famous theatre in Hollywood where movie stars stood in wet concrete so that forever after anyone passing, seeing their footprints, would know they were famous.

Lincoln wondered if the concrete was dry. It looked as hard as the fudge Sassy sometimes made. He didn't think it would hurt to pretend to be writing something on the very edge. Something important like: "Herman, the famous Astronaut, brother of Lincoln."

Lincoln set his books down, found a stick, knelt down and pretended he was writing. Well, for goodness sake, the concrete was soft. He *was* writing. Now he'd started he'd better finish. He wasn't sure he knew how to spell "astronaut" so he wrote "flyer."

Then he stood up and examined his work. At that moment a heavy hand grasped his jacket, practically lifting Lincoln off his feet, and choking him. He looked up into the face of a huge man carrying a trowel.

"Uhuh! A defacer!" the huge man roared. "I've always wanted to catch a defacer in the act."

Lincoln didn't know what a defacer was, but he didn't

25

think he wanted to be one. "I was just testing the concrete, to see if it was hard."

"You had to write your whole name to make sure?"

"It's not my name," Lincoln gasped. "It's my brother's."

The huge man bent over and read what Lincoln had written. "Herman, the flyer, is your brother?" he asked.

Lincoln nodded. "He will be when he's born."

The man's jaw dropped. "He's a flyer and he isn't even born?"

"My mom went to the hospital this morning," Lincoln said. "Herman's going to be an astronaut."

The man loosened his grip. "Suppose you get a sister?"

"I've already got three," Lincoln said. "Besides four girl cousins, and our street is overcrowded with girls."

The man let go of Lincoln. "I see your problem," he said, rubbing his jaw.

He looked down at Lincoln's writing again. "I really ought to smooth Herman over, but since he's just on the

Helmsh, the famous flier, prefers o

very edge, I suppose I could let him be. Then you'd have a brother, in concrete at least."

Lincoln grinned. "Thank you, mister," he said.

"Now you'd better beat it, and, mind you, you walk straight to school."

Lincoln walked so straight he felt stiff-legged.

He wasn't even late.

And now he had a really famous brother. He could hardly wait for the day to go by so he could run home and tell the family.

But no one would be there. He felt kind of quivery thinking about it.

Maybe he hadn't understood Mrs. Readywell. Maybe she'd be there waiting.

4

BUT OF COURSE Mrs. Readywell wasn't there.

Lincoln got the key from the secret place, behind the loose brick by the mailbox, and unlocked the door. He had never been in the apartment when it was so still. He pretended he was a railroad train highballing it to Washington. He ran from the engine to the caboose, making a noise like a Diesel. It sounded lonely in the empty rooms. Without changing from his school clothes he went out into the hall and down the back way to the basement, where he got his basketball out of the closet.

In the little square in back of the apartment he started shooting baskets. He pretended he was Uncle Jay making the famous play that had won the championship for his school. Uncle Jay said Lincoln had a good right arm. Now Lincoln shot three baskets in a row. *Zowie!* Only there was no one to see. Not even the tomcats.

He decided to go out front where there was more excitement.

He sat on the stoop for a while, then he walked to the corner, past some girls playing jump-the-rope, and more girls showing off on roller skates. It felt good to be on his own without his sisters bossing him, telling him to change his clothes, or go wash his face, or something.

Of course, later, when he was sure Uncle Jay was home from work, he'd have to telephone Aunt Charlotte's. He'd talk to Uncle Jay and tell him the whole story about Mrs. Readywell. It would be different from telling it to Aunt Charlotte, who got excited over the least little thing Lincoln said. Uncle Jay would come over and maybe sleep in Pop's bed, but first they'd shoot a few baskets and Uncle Jay would show Lincoln once more just how he made that champion shot. But Uncle Jay wouldn't be home from work for quite a while yet.

Lincoln crossed the street. He walked past the Savings

and Loan Bank on the corner, past the delicatessen and the Laundromat. He stopped in front of the grocery store and leaned against the window. He felt so free he thought he could fly. He was an eagle soaring high as a jet. He pumped his arms up and down and the wind and clouds brushed his face.

At that moment, a man, with his coat collar turned up and his hat brim turned down, came hurrying down the street. He tossed a brown paper sack into Lincoln's outstretched wings, and shoved some bills into his fist. "There's more where this came from if you'll take my lunch to the subway corner and wait for me," the man said over his shoulder as he flashed out of sight in the crowd.

Lincoln clutched the bag and looked at the money. The man had given him three five-dollar bills. *Zowie!* Lincoln took off like a fire engine. Behind him he heard a clatter of bells. When he was halfway down the street a police car screamed by.

At the subway stairs Lincoln waited and waited.

After a while, Officer Roberts arrived, all business and no nonsense, the way he was when he had no time for jokes. "What you hanging around for, son?" he asked.

"I'm waiting for a man to pick up his lunch," Lincoln said, holding up the sack.

"Well, it's way past lunchtime," Officer Roberts said. "Now you get along home."

Pop was a stickler about doing exactly as Officer Roberts said, so Lincoln went home.

He let himself into the house, walked to the kitchen and plunked the sack down on the table. It began to split. Before his eyes, bundles of greenbacks spilled on the table.

Was he dreaming? Lincoln closed his eyes, then opened them slowly.

He was surrounded by money.

He took three steps forward, then three steps sideways, and looked again.

It was still money.

Zowie! What would Officer Roberts say about this?

Quickly, he emptied his book bag and stuffed the money, torn sack and all, into it. Then he highballed it out of the house. He did remember to put the key back.

At the subway corner, Officer Roberts was untangling traffic. Lincoln held up the bag. "It's filled with money," he cried.

Officer Roberts was having troubles. He was blowing his

whistle at a lady jaywalker, and at the same time he was trying to stop a dogfight. A police car whined down the street and stopped right next to him.

"Officer Roberts . . ." Lincoln cried. "Officer Roberts."

Officer Roberts waved Lincoln away. "Now see here, young man, I'm too busy to listen to your yarns today. Away with you and don't you dare let me catch you back here again."

Well! Money belonged in a bank, Lincoln knew that. It must be almost closing time. He raced down the street and around the corner. A guard was just pulling the doors closed.

Lincoln held up the bag. "It's money."

The guard shrugged, pointed to the closing time on the window, and pulled down the shade.

5

LINCOLN stopped to think. What should he do now? If he took the money to Aunt Charlotte's, she'd probably faint. Still, he couldn't just walk around with it, for Uncle Jay to get home from work.

Now, if only Sara were here. He was used to her being in charge when Pop and Mom were not at home. She was bossy but she did know the right thing to do.

But Sara was on her way to Washington.

No, she wasn't! Not yet! Her train wasn't to leave until sometime after school was out. If he rushed to the station he'd probably be just in time to see her.

As he made a dash for the subway stairs, Lincoln saw that Officer Roberts was busier than ever. He was talking with two policemen now. They pointed this way and that. They shook their heads. They wrote things down.

Lincoln knew about subways. Often on Sundays after church Pop took the family to places like the United Nations or Rockefeller Center. Always, he gave the children the money to pay the fares. It was more fun that way.

So Lincoln knew how to get places. He went to the change booth and with one of the five-dollar bills he bought some tokens, then dropped one in the turnstile, and swung aboard the subway.

The Washington train was being called when Lincoln burst into the station. He rushed this way and that, skidding over the floor, looking for Sara. He remembered that she was wearing a blue dress this morning so he chased after every blue dress in sight. But Sara just wasn't around anywhere. Well, he thought, it was just like her to have been the very first one to board the train.

Over the loudspeaker now he heard the last call for the Washington train. He squirreled through the line headed for the gate, peering up into faces. He was carried along by the crowd right through the gate and, for goodness sakes, there was the train. He sprinted onto the last car and rushed from coach to coach looking for Sara. He reached the very last one, a real old-timer. But Sara wasn't in Old-Timer either. Come to think about it, Lincoln hadn't seen any sign of a high school group on the train.

Then he remembered. Sara's train was an excursion, which meant it would probably follow this regular train and was still in the station.

Outside now he heard: *"All aboard."*

He dashed for the vestibule.

The train began to move. It picked up speed. He stood there with his heart pounding and his skin crawling while New York vanished. His legs felt wobbly and all hollow when he finally stumbled back inside Old-Timer and collapsed on the nearest seat.

He was headed for Washington. Alone. And he had this sack of money he didn't know what to do with. The world was zipping by a mile a minute and his head felt as if it were whirling on a nonstop merry-go-round.

Was this really happening to him, Lincoln Farnum? Maybe he was imagining it all. Maybe his imagination had got stuck, like a needle on a phonograph record, and couldn't get unstuck, and he was really back home in the

37

apartment and his school bag was filled with books and peanut-butter sandwiches. He opened it and looked. It was still money. Reaching in, he took out one of the stacks and examined a bill. Abraham Lincoln's picture was on it. THE UNITED STATES OF AMERICA, WASHINGTON, D.C., he read.

That made him feel better. Mr. Lincoln was his special friend, and the money was headed back in the direction from which it had come in the first place. In a way, it was as if he were on official business for Mr. Lincoln. And besides, Sara was on a train right behind this one. He'd wait for her in the Washington station, and when she learned about the money she would know at once what to do.

As he slipped the money back into the bag, Lincoln noticed the man sitting across the aisle. He was reading a newspaper and he was wearing black glasses. Lincoln's favorite television show was *The Spy in the Sky*. The spy traveled by airplane and he always wore black glasses. Now the man looked up from his newspaper and stared straight across the aisle at Lincoln. Lincoln couldn't see the man's eyes because of the glasses, but on television when the spy took his glasses off his eyes were dark and piercing. Actually, they were X-ray eyes that looked straight through his victim and read his thoughts.

Quick as a flash, Lincoln looked away and dropped the bag of money to the floor and planted his feet firmly on it.

He was a special courier in Mr. Lincoln's army and he had this dispatch case filled with valuable papers to deliver to Mr. Lincoln in Washington. The enemy was all around, plotting to get the papers. Lincoln bent over, to make sure the papers hadn't disappeared from under his feet, just as a pair of black shoes advanced along the aisle and halted alongside the dispatch case. The shoes were attached to legs in uniform. Lincoln thought about drawing his rifle and rattling his saber, but he couldn't move, he was frozen scared, bent over like a pretzel.

A voice roared above him: "TICKET PLEASE!"

Ticket?

Lincoln's head snapped up like a jack-in-the-box. Would they put him off the train? Take him to jail? He blinked and looked up into the pink face of the conductor; he swallowed, trying to unstick his voice.

"Where are your folks, boy?" the conductor prodded. "Do they have your ticket?"

Lincoln shook his head.

The man in the dark glasses leaned across the aisle and laughed. "Maybe you've got another runaway, John."

The conductor pursed his lips and raised his eyebrows. "So you've got no ticket ànd no folks?"

Lincoln's voice came back in a rush. "I have too got folks — Mom and Pop, and there's Sissy and Sassy, and Herman-to-be, and I'm going to meet my sister Sara in Washington, and I've got money to pay my fare."

"Well then," the conductor said. "I'll have five dollars and thirty-three cents, please."

Lincoln reached into his pockets and counted out the money.

"I should charge you ten cents extra for not having a ticket," the conductor said. "Buy yourself a coke — the railroad's treat."

Lincoln grinned and thanked the nice conductor.

The man in the black glasses reached across the aisle and handed Lincoln a package of gum. He took off his

glasses. His eyes were blue and friendly. He wasn't a spy after all.

Lincoln was just a little disappointed at this. But then he took his feet off the military secrets and began to enjoy his adventure. Imagine him, Lincoln Farnum, headed for Washington, and his sister Sara on a train right behind him not knowing a thing about it.

Pop called his train "my home on wheels," and Lincoln thought how cozy it was sitting here in Old-Timer as it clickety-clacked through new and exciting scenes.

When the sandwich man came through the car, Lincoln bought two hot dogs, a coke, and some candy.

This surely was more exciting than running through the apartment pretending he was on a train. This was real. He hummed to the "clickety-clack" tune of the rails. Later it changed to "clack-clack-C L A C K." Old-Timer had what Pop called "flat feet." One of its wheels was giving up. Maybe they'd be late getting in.

They were.

Already the sky was darkening. Why, Washington was a big city. Lincoln always thought of New York as giant and every other place as little.

He got goose bumps. His mouth went dry.

What was he worried about? Sara was following close behind.

When the train pulled into the station he was the first one off. He ran all the way to the inside and asked a train-man at which gate the excursion would come in.

"No more excursions tonight," the man told him. "There was one in about half an hour ago.

Sara's train had left ahead of the regular, not after. He had been stupid not to think of that. He'd never find her tonight.

Now what would he do?

Where should he go? Where could he sleep?

Lincoln was scared.

How much of his fifteen dollars did he have left? He dug into his pockets. He counted. He had exactly eight dollars and sixty-seven cents. *Money!* In his rush to get off the train and look for Sara, Lincoln had forgotten the bag. He had left Mr. Lincoln's bills back there in Old-Timer.

6

Lincoln raced back to the train.

It was still standing in the same place, but now it was empty. He ran straight to Old-Timer and dashed for his seat. The canvas bag was exactly as he had left it. Just as he reached down to grasp it, the train gave a sharp jerk. Lincoln went sprawling into the aisle.

He scrambled to his feet.

The train was moving.

Bump! Bump! STOP.

Lincoln spun around like a top and landed across a seat.

"Ding! Ding!" Now they were going backwards.

BUMP!

The engine was switching, getting rid of its tail of cars. Soon Old-Timer was the only one left.

Ding Ding! Old-Timer was backed into a barnlike place.

BUMP! The engine went off by itself, leaving Old-Timer and Lincoln alone.

Men in overalls came and stood around the coach. Lincoln shrank back into his seat, but the men didn't look up into the windows. They looked down at the wheels. They crawled under Old-Timer.

BANG! Lincoln shot up a foot. He peeked out the window. Some of the men carried flashlights. They were working on Old-Timer's flat feet with hammers and torches and wrenches.

The men talked and laughed while they worked. They were railroad men. Pop was a railroad man. As Lincoln listened to their voices he began to get drowsy. Pop said there was no better place to sleep than on a train. Lincoln made a pillow out of the bag of money and closed his eyes.

When he opened them it was light. Watery light.

Swish! Swish! Swish!

What was that? He sat bolt upright. He was under water but he wasn't wet. Where was he?

45

He came fully awake. He was in Old-Timer. A mop appeared at the window. Old-Timer was getting a bath. Next the cleaners would probably come into the coach. He had to get out. It was morning in Washington and he must find Sara.

Lincoln slung the bag of money over his shoulder and, when no one was looking, hopped off the coach and headed for the station, where he washed up extra clean in the rest room. Sara would throw a fit if he didn't look right.

Then he went into the coffee shop and bought himself a good breakfast — a hamburger and a milk shake. Now he felt ready for anything. Why, he'd find Sara without any trouble. She had said her group would probably go to the White House first thing. She'd be gawking at the sights and he'd bump smack into her. She'd tell him what to do about the money, and then after that he'd walk right into the White House and up the stairs to Mr. Lincoln's bedroom, and then after that he'd see the Lincoln Memorial, and after that he'd have to catch the train in order to get home before Mrs. Readywell arrived to take care of him.

But first he had to find the White House.

Pop always said only two kinds of people were worth asking how to get places: taxi drivers and policemen.

There were no taxis about when Lincoln came out of the station, but he did see a long black car with a chauffeur standing alongside, so he walked right up and asked for directions.

The chauffeur grinned and pointed. "Right over there

in front of the station you can get on a bus marked FRIEND-
SHIP HEIGHTS. You just missed one."

A man carrying a briefcase came hurrying.

"Good morning, Senator," the chauffeur said, opening
the car door.

Then the chauffeur turned back to Lincoln. "There'll be
another bus soon. It isn't very far to the White House."

The Senator leaned out the door. "I'm going to see the
President. The boy can ride with us."

And so Lincoln stepped into the shiny black limousine
and sat down right next to the Senator.

7

AND THAT'S HOW Lincoln went to the White House.

Things happened to Lincoln that never happened to anyone else. If he told Sissy and Sassy that he saw Washington from a magic pumpkin, all painted shiny black, they'd laugh their heads off.

The Senator was very smart. Without asking any questions, he guessed right away that Lincoln had never before been to Washington. He pointed out the Capitol Building standing strong and high on the Hill. He asked the chauffeur to swing around so Lincoln could see the Washington Monument, and the Lincoln Memorial, grave and thoughtful in the distance.

Lincoln looked left and right trying to see all the famous places.

And then they were at the White House.

After he said good-bye to the Senator and to the chauffeur, Lincoln just stood there looking at his White House. He peered through the high gates and he saw that his house was shining white and stood in a green park with singing fountains. Bright flowers lined the walks, and trees shaded the grass. Lincoln felt so proud of his house he got a funny feeling in his chest like when he saw the Stars and Stripes go by in a parade.

Already a line had begun to form. Lincoln walked up and down the sidewalk looking for Sara. He realized that finding her wasn't going to be so easy. There were crowds of children and teen-agers. Groups of grown-ups. People dressed in their church clothes, and others who looked as if they were camping, came walking, or in cars, or in taxis. The cars had license plates from states far and near.

The visitors had all kinds of voices — soft-as-velvet kind, and the kind that twanged like Uncle Jay's guitar. There were slow and careful voices, as if the words were still new to the speakers and each one must be thought about separately.

A column of Boy Scouts came marching — hip — hip — hip. Lincoln got in line right behind them.

A band played in the distance. Three airplanes roared overhead. A high school group poured out of a bus. The boys wore beanies with WASHINGTON on them, and the girls wore head scarves decorated with Washington scenes. This reminded Lincoln to look for Sara. But he couldn't leave the line or he'd lose his place.

"We're moving," someone shouted, and the line hushed and went forward through the tall gates, past the guards, and up the curving walk.

When Lincoln walked through the big doors of the White House he had the feeling that his feet were not touching the pavement and his head was a balloon floating in midair.

At home, Lincoln had a tube-shaped toy called a kaleidoscope that held loose bits of colored glass. When he looked through one end of it, the glass pieces reflected against mirrors and made pretty patterns. Now Lincoln felt as if he were in a giant kaleidoscope as he walked through the beautiful rooms. Color patterns kept exploding

at each turning. The colors went from gold to green to blue to red.

The patterns formed chandeliers of diamonds, floors like mirrors, candles and flowers. There were square rooms; oval rooms; velvets and satins. Paintings of past Presidents and First Ladies. Benjamin Franklin's picture, all life and color, was in the Green Room; the bare floor of the Blue Room was polished to a high shine and made Lincoln's feet itch to do a jig, but he'd never sit on Dolly Madison's sofa in the Red Room. It was for storybook ladies in rustly silks and laces. There was so much to see so swiftly. Lincoln tried to make memories of the patterns before each new burst of color.

The dining room, all white and gold, was so big Lincoln thought that even if all his relations came to dinner they wouldn't half fill it.

But the best was yet to come. All of this was leading up to the moment when he would see his bedroom.

The line moved out into the wide, red-carpeted hall. Now Lincoln saw that the great stairway leading to the next floor was roped off, and the line was moving toward the outside. He hesitated. A guard motioned him on. "But we didn't see Lincoln's bedroom," Lincoln said.

"We have about ten thousand visitors, and just two hours' time," the guard said.

"But my name is Lincoln, and I came all the way from New York."

"Some of these tourists are from Alaska and California and foreign lands," the guard said. "Here, you can have this guidebook. It has a nice picture of Lincoln's bedroom."

Lincoln thanked the guard and followed the crowd outside and through the gates. He stood looking back at his White House. He had not seen his bedroom. He had not found Sara.

Now the pack on his back felt heavy.

He had been foolish to think he would find Sara in such a big city. She had said that Washington belonged to the people. They were surely taking it over; crowds pressing into this place and that. Time was pressing, too. He had very little of it left before he must be on a train going home. But he couldn't leave without trying to see the Lincoln Memorial. It would probably be like Lincoln's bedroom; he wouldn't get anywhere near it.

And then he'd have to go straight to the police station. It was what he should have been smart enough to do in the first place. They would ask him all kinds of questions; they'd hold him, maybe in a jail cell; they'd call Pop.

Lincoln started walking. He thought about how he had

not performed as Pop would like, as an engineer who knew where he was going and how to get there.

Pop called the caboose on his train "the Clown Wagon." Lincoln guessed that was where he really belonged — in the Clown Wagon.

He felt ashamed. Sissy and Sassy would never stop laughing. "Imagine Lincoln taking a sack of money from a stranger and really believing it was sandwiches," they would say.

Sara would be impatient. "Imagine Lincoln following me all the way to Washington . . ."

And poor Pop, who taught his family to do right, would look as if he'd allowed Lincoln to run wild, like a handcar going downhill without brakes.

Aunt Charlotte would have a good faint, and Uncle Jay would ask how he expected to be a top basketball player if he didn't use his head.

And Herman . . . Lincoln didn't want Herman ever to find out he had such a stupid brother. Maybe it would be just as well if the baby turned out to be a Hermione.

And then Lincoln reached the Lincoln Memorial.

When he looked up into the face of the great figure, he knew all at once that the President had been waiting for him, for he sat relaxed in his chair, his expression kindly, unhurried.

In all of busy, crowded Washington, the President had time. Lincoln told him about his troubles, silently of course, and the President listened most attentively. In the misty light about his face, his lips seemed to move in answer. "You have been brave to come such a long way alone, Lincoln Farnum, and I thank you."

Courier Lincoln Farnum of the Union Army stood proudly and saluted his Commander in Chief.

And now, across the Courier's vision, strode a man wearing black glasses.

A spy!

"The papers," Lincoln seemed to say, his arms outstretched.

In one quick movement, Courier Lincoln Farnum slid the bag with its military secrets from his shoulder. He tossed it high — a perfect arc — like Uncle Jay's championship shot. It came to rest at the President's feet.

And then, before the onlookers grasped what had happened, Lincoln ran down into the crowd. He stood there grinning as people shouted and pointed to the sack, and guards swarmed about.

And then, for goodness sakes, if he didn't see Sara. She was with her class, walking toward the monument, so close to Lincoln he could have reached out and touched her. Instead, he ducked. He had taken care of matters himself.

Who was in charge of Lincoln?

Lincoln.

One day he would come back to Washington, when he was big so he wouldn't have to worry about grown-ups worrying about him. He would stay as long a time as he needed to see everything — the Eternal Flame — the Pentagon — the Senate in session. But now he must go home.

8

Mrs. Readywell was just unlocking the door when Lincoln reached home.

"Hello, boy," she said. "Guess I'm just in time to take care of you. No one being home, I figured your mom went to the hospital today."

"You're late, a day late," Lincoln said. "She went yesterday."

"What's that you say?" Mrs. Readywell asked.

Lincoln knew there was no use explaining. She'd never get it straight.

Mrs. Readywell went right into the kitchen to start dinner. "Your pop will be home soon," she said.

Lincoln collapsed on the sofa.

The next thing he knew, Sissy and Sassy were rushing into the apartment, talking a blue streak, telling about Aunt Charlotte's banana cake, and about Uncle Jay buying everybody double malteds, on and on and on.

Sassy had brought in the evening newspaper and was opening it.

Sissy came to stand in front of Lincoln. "And what did you do?" she asked.

"I went to Washington to see Mr. Lincoln," he said.

Sassy grinned. "I suppose you slept in his bed."

"Didn't even see it, but I did have a long talk with him."

"And what did you use for money to get there?" Sissy asked.

Sassy rustled the newspaper. "Simple," she said. "Lincoln found a big bag of it."

Lincoln spun around. How had they found out? Had Sara seen him after all? Was she home? Or had she telephoned?

Sassy laughed and pointed to the headline in the newspaper. She read aloud:

N.Y. BANK HAUL TURNS UP IN WASHINGTON
WHO TOSSED THE LOOT TO LINCOLN?

"I suppose you're going to say you did," Sissy said.

"Yep," Lincoln said.

"When are you going to stop telling tall tales?" Sassy asked.

Suddenly Lincoln knew when. *Now!*

After yesterday and today, he could never imagine anything as fantastic as what had really happened.

There was a key in the lock. Pop came into the room beaming. "Well, what do you think we've got?" he asked.

"A sister, a sister," the twins cried.

Lincoln was afraid to hope, but Pop grinned at him. "A brother," he said.

A brother! At last, a brother!

Herman!

One day he would tell Herman about his trip to Washington. Herman wouldn't laugh at him. Herman would believe.

Zowie!

The Author

DALE FIFE lives with her family in San Mateo, California, where she spends a good deal of time writing. She is the author of both adult novels and stories for young readers. *Who's in Charge of Lincoln?* is her second book for boys and girls.

A Stork for the Bell Tower, Dale Fife's first book, was set in Alsace which is one of her special interests, for both her parents were born there. She has done a great deal of research on Alsace and she actually lived for a time in the little village where her mother grew up.

Of *A Stork for the Bell Tower*, the *Horn Book* says: "Alsatian mood and customs are dominant with delightful glimpses of regional attitudes and atmosphere. The pictures give the color sensation of blueberries on black raspberry mousse — unusual and very French!"

The Artist

PAUL GALDONE was born in Budapest, Hungary, but he has lived in the United States since he was fourteen years old.

Mr. Galdone studied at the Art Students League of New York. He has illustrated many fine books for boys and girls. He now makes his home in Rockland County, New York.

DATE DUE

RETURNED
RETURNED
RETURNED

MAR 0 7 1977

WITHDRAWN FROM
OHIO NORTHERN
UNIVERSITY LIBRARY

GAYLORD

PRINTED IN U.S.A.

BENJAMIN ELKIN has been telling stories all his life, first to his own nine brothers and sisters, and then to the other children on the block in his native Baltimore. Now principal of the Rogers Elementary School in Chicago, Mr. Elkin is the author of more than a dozen books for children. Four of these have been chosen as Junior Literary Guild Selections. He is the author of *Lucky and the Giant, Al and the Magic Lamp,* and *The Beginners Book of Magic,* scheduled for 1966 publication.

In 1965 Mr. Elkin received a special Citation of Merit from the National Association for Gifted Children for his contributions to quality education through curriculum enrichment.

JEROME SNYDER, the art director of *Scientific American,* has been involved with the graphic arts ever since leaving school. His awards and citations range from the American Institute of Graphic Arts right up to the United States Government. Among his other books are *Umbrellas, Hats and Wheels,* and *One Day in Ancient Rome.* At present he lives in Brooklyn with his wife and two sons.

WHY THE SUN WAS LATE

By
BENJAMIN ELKIN

Illustrated by
JEROME SNYDER

Parents' Magazine Press
New York

It was a lazy afternoon. In the jungle
an old, weak tree waited for just one small breeze
to make it fall. But the air was calm
and there was no breeze.

Then along came a buzzing fly. He stopped to rest
on a leaf of the old tree. And that one touch
was enough. The tired tree gave a sigh, and then
toppled over with a crash.

Buzz! said the amazed fly. "Who would have
guessed that I, by myself alone, would be
strong enough to knock down a tree?"
And, puffed up with pride, he flew away
to see what else he could do.

Soon the fly saw two boys climbing another tree
to gather nuts. "Here's where I have some fun,"
thought the fly. "Won't those boys be surprised
when I push them right off the tree!"

The fly buzzed from one boy to the other,
trying to make them fall. But the mighty strength
that had knocked down the tree seemed to be gone.
All the fly could do was tickle them on the nose.

"Oh, go away!" said one of the boys.
He swung wildly at the fly with his hand.
But instead of hitting the fly he hit a branch.
And that blow really started something...

It so happened that three squirrels
had been sitting on that very same branch.
Down fell the three squirrels. And they landed
right on top of four snakes who were
sleeping in the grass.

The four startled snakes jumped up.
They slithered off in the grass without
stopping to look. And they blundered into
a herd of five elephants.

The five elephants trumpeted with fear.
They rushed madly across the field. Crash!
They bumped headfirst into a hill. The trees
on the hill swayed and trembled. And out of
one tree fell a nest with six eggs.

Then the poor mother bird began to cry.
"Oh, my darling babies. Their shells are cracked.
Now my heart is broken, too. Never, never, never
shall I sing again."

All that afternoon and all that night,
the mother bird was silent. At last it was
time for dawn, but the bird did not sing
her usual wake-up song. Now everyone knows
it's the song of a bird that wakes the sun.
Without that song, the sun slept on and on.
And the day was as dark as night.

The animals looked longingly for the sun.
Hopefully, they waited and waited. But not one
ray of light did they see. At last they cried out

to the Great Spirit. And the Great Spirit gave ear to their cries. He called all the animals together.

"Tell me, oh bird," said the Great Spirit.
"Why did you not sing and wake the sun?"

"How can I ever sing again?" asked
the unhappy bird. "My heart is broken.
My six lovely eggs were cracked by those
five elephants."

"Pardon, Great Spirit," said the five elephants.
"We did not mean to do it. All five of us
were frightened by those four snakes."

"It was not our fault," said the four snakes.
"We were sleeping peacefully. Suddenly
those three squirrels landed right on top of us."

"But we couldn't help it," said the squirrels.
"The three of us were tumbled out of a tree
by those two boys."

"That was purely an accident." said the boys.
"The two of us were buzzed at and buzzed at
by that one pesky fly. He tried to make us fall."

"Let me see if I have this right,"
said the Great Spirit.

"The six eggs...
were broken by the five elephants...
who were frightened by the four snakes...
who were startled by the three squirrels...
who were tumbled down by the two boys...
who were buzzed at by one fly.

"So it seems to have begun with you, oh fly.
Tell me. Why did you buzz at the two boys?"

The fly did not know what to say. How could he
admit in front of everyone that he thought
he had knocked down a tree all by himself, alone?
So all he said was *Buzz, Buzz, Buzz.*

"Come, come," said the Great Spirit. "You can speak as plainly as the others. Tell me why you buzzed at the boys."

Buzz, Buzz, Buzz, said the fly.

"I shall give you just one more chance to explain," said the Great Spirit.

Buzz, Buzz, Buzz, said the fly.
And not one other word would he say.

"So be it," said the Great Spirit. "You would not speak when I asked you to. So you shall never speak again. From now on you shall say nothing but *Buzz, Buzz, Buzz*."

Then the Great Spirit smiled kindly at the
mother bird. "When you return to your nest,
you will find your six eggs whole again," he said.
"Now, my child, sing and wake the sun."

"Oh, thank you," said the grateful bird.
She sang a beautiful wake-up call.
A rosy color appeared in the sky.
And the sun got up at last.

The mother bird returned to the hill.
She found her six eggs safely back in the nest.
So she happily cuddled them again.

The five elephants contentedly returned
to their own places in the field.

The four snakes went back to sleep in the grass.

The three squirrels chattered away on their
very own branch.

The two boys went back to gathering nuts
in the tree.

And the fly returned to his buzzing in the
forest. Only this time he was careful to choose
a strong young tree upon which to rest.

Since that day the mother bird has faithfully called the sun every morning. That is why the sun has never been late again.

And since that day the silly fly has never spoken another word.

All he can say is *Buzz, Buzz, Buzz.*